A Grey Bear with a Blue Nose

The Me to You Story

• Me to You •

First published by Carte Blanche Greetings Ltd 2003
First published in this format by HarperCollins Children's Books in 2009
1 3 5 7 9 10 8 6 4 2
ISBN-13: 978-0-00-731500-0
A CIP Catalogue record for this title is available from the British Library.

www.harpercollins.co.uk

www.carteblanchegreetings.com

Printed and bound in China

A Grey Bear with a Blue Nose

The Me to You Story

Illustrated by Steve Mort-Hill

HarperCollins *Children's Books*

The oldest, smallest house you can imagine
was about to be knocked down.

All the things that once made the house nice and
cosy had been thrown outside and piled up
in the front garden, from the soft springy bed,
to the old wooden floorboards.

And even,
surely by some mistake,
a little brown teddy bear.

He was trapped amongst all the other
unwanted things and couldn't move.

Then, one day, a very, very cold day,
something fell from the sky.

A small snowflake.

It landed on the teddy bear's nose,
and was then followed by many more.

The little bear was now so cold that his nose
started turning blue…so cold that his brown
fur started turning grey.

He was cold, unloved and
all alone in the world,
and he felt very, very sad.

Winter finally passed and the weather got warmer. Then, one beautiful spring day, a little girl was playing near the old house, when she spotted the grey bear in a pile of unwanted things.

He was like no other bear she had ever seen.

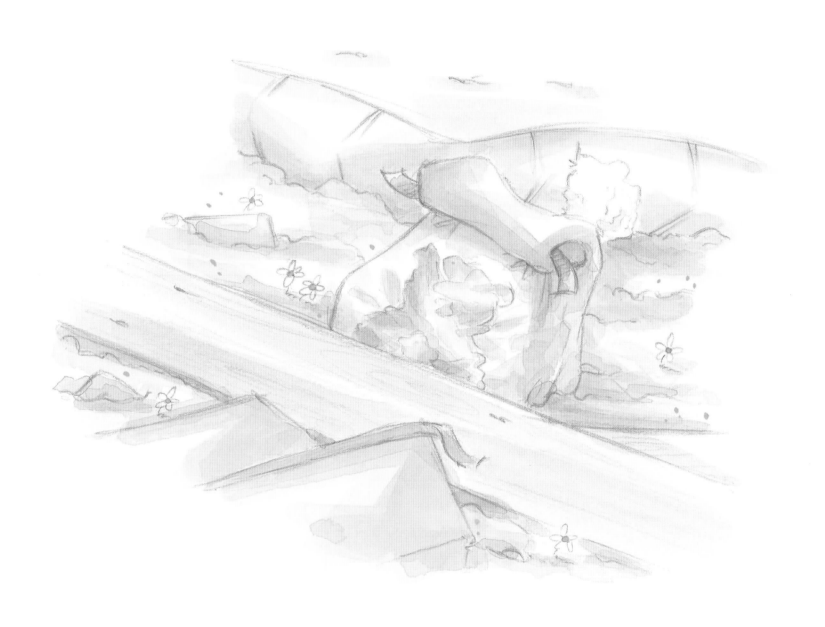

She pulled him out from the rubbish

that trapped him.

She dusted him down and lifted him high in the sky to look at him. The teddy bear wanted to cry. He thought she didn't like him and would throw him back with all the other unwanted things.

But she didn't.

"He's lovely!" she continued,
and she fell completely
in love with him.

She ran home as fast as
her little legs could carry her.

She wanted to see if her Grandma could
patch him up, as a lot of his stuffing had fallen
out and he was very much in need of repair.

She looked on as her
Grandma replaced his stuffing and
patched up his holes.

His stitches had started showing
where the fur had worn away,
but the little girl thought
he looked perfect.

It was all cosy and warm in the little girl's house and the bear now felt cosy and warm in his heart. However, his nose was still blue and his fur was still grey and they would never return to brown, but he was unique amongst teddy bears.

The little girl gave him a great big hug, placed a kiss on his blue nose and whispered, "From Me to You".

She loved him more than anything
else in the world, her little, grey,
blue-nosed Tatty Teddy.